A Break-of-Day Book

Ever since 1928, when Wanda Gág's classic *Millions of Cats* appeared, Coward-McCann has been publishing books of high quality for young readers. Among them are the easy-to-read stories known as Break-of-Day books. This series appears under the colophon shown above — a rooster crowing in the sunrise — which is adapted from one of Wanda Gág's illustrations for *Tales from Grimm*.

Though the language used in Break-of-Day books is deliberately kept as clear and as simple as possible, the stories are not written in a controlled vocabulary. And while chosen to be within the grasp of readers in the primary grades, their content is far-ranging and varied enough to captivate children who have just begun crossing the momentous threshold into the world of books.

Commander Toad

and the

DIS-ASTEROID

by Jane Yolen

Pictures by
Bruce Degen

Coward-McCann, Inc.
New York

For Graham and the H. (Hip & Hop) Roberts

Text copyright © 1985 by Jane Yolen
Illustrations copyright © 1985 by Bruce Degen
All rights reserved. This book, or parts thereof, may
not be reproduced in any form without permission in
writing from the publishers. Published simultaneously
in Canada by General Publishing Co. Limited, Toronto.
Third hardcover impression
Second paperback impression
Printed in the United States of America
Library of Congress Cataloging in Publication Data
Yolen, Jane.
Commander Toad & the dis-asteroid.
Summary: Commander Toad and his spaceship Star Warts
answer a mysterious call for help from a flooded asteroid.
[1. Science fiction. 2. Toads—Fiction] I. Degen,
Bruce, ill. II. Title. III. Title: Commander Toad
and the dis-asteroid.
PZ7.Y78Cg 1985 [E] 84-1897
ISBN 0-698-30744-5
ISBN 0-698-20620-7 pbk.
Printed in the United States of America

To those constant Apanage Readers:
     the exHOPtional Andrew Sigel
     Jim the Peeper Macdonald
     Ian Tadpole Duncan
     David Warts-and-All Hulan
     Bruce Faithful Toad Coville
     Rich Webby Morrissey
     Dave Hoperator Locke
     Jymn Little Hop Magon
     and
     The Big HOPfner

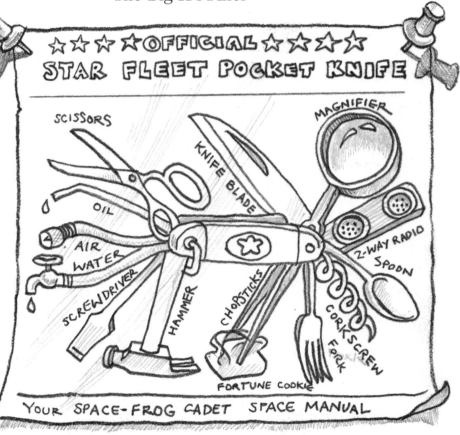

Long green ships
fly between the stars.
All across the galaxy
worlds wink off and on.
There is one ship,
one mighty ship,
filled with a topflight crew.
The captain of this ship
is brave and bright,
bright and brave.
He is the hero
of the fleet.
His name is
COMMANDER TOAD.

His long green ship
is called *Star Warts*.
It goes where no space ship
has gone before.
To find planets.
To explore galaxies.
To bring a little bit of Earth
out to the alien stars.

Commander Toad
has a very fine crew.
His copilot
is Mr. Hop
who thinks and thinks.
His engineer
is Lieutenant Lily
who tinkers and tinkers.
His computer chief
is young Jake Skyjumper
who reads and reads.

And then there is
old Doc Peeper
in his grass-green wig.
Everyone is hoppiest
when Doc has nothing
at all to do.

Today's mission
is a simple one.
As the ship
is ready to leave
its Star Fleet base,
Commander Toad
calls the crew together.
"Star Fleet
has heard an SOS,"
says Commander Toad.

"There has been
a disaster
on a world between
Jupiter and Mars.
That world
is an asteroid."
Lieutenant Lily
raises her hand.
"What kind of disaster?"
she asks.

"We are not sure.
The message is strange.
Read it, Mr. Hop,"
says Commander Toad.
Mr. Hop
clears his throat
of the frog in it.
He reads:
"Help. Help.
Beans swell.
Beans bad."

13

"What does that mean?"
asks young Jake,
scratching his head.
"We think it means
their bean crop
did not grow
even though
they had very good beans,"
says Mr. Hop.

"Star Fleet
wants us to deliver
a whole new hold
full of swell beans,"
says Commander Toad.
Young Jake
checks the computer.
"Look at all the beans
that have been
put on board."

15

They read off the list:
Black beans,
French beans,
Green beans,
Jelly beans,
Jumping beans,
Runner beans,
String beans,
Yellow beans.
"Those *are* swell beans,"
says Doc Peeper.

Commander Toad
points to the map
that shimmers on the wall.
"If we do not
bring the beans
to the good folk
on that asteroid,
it will be
a *dis-asteroid*.
We must get there
as fast as we can."

So they all
hop to work.
Lieutenant Lily
sets the engines
on full speed ahead.
Mr. Hop
plots their course.
Young Jake Skyjumper
checks the computer.
Old Doc Peeper
keeps an eye on them all.

And what does
Commander Toad do?
He watches for danger
in deep hopper space.
He is a hero,
after all.
It is a hero's job
to be brave and bright,
bright and brave,
and to know
just when to worry.

Suddenly something
pings across the nose
of the ship.
"Do not worry,"
says Commander Toad.
"It is only
a shooting star.
They have very bad aim."

The ship goes on.
Suddenly something
moos in front of it.
"Do not worry,"
says Commander Toad.
"It is only
a cow jumping
over the moon.
That is how we got
the Milky Way."

21

"We are not worried,"
says the crew.
"You are a hero,
Commander Toad.
You will tell us
when to worry.
That is your job."
The ship goes on
because Commander Toad
is not worried yet.
He is too busy
looking out for danger.
He is so busy looking,
he does not know danger
when he sees it.

Ahead on the screen
is a pleasant world.
It is filled with water.
There are no cities,
no houses,
no bus stops or barns.
Just water
everywhere.
Above the water,
calling softly
as they fly,
are thousands of doves.

"What a pretty world,"
says Commander Toad.
But young Jake
comes jumping forward.
He has a star map
in his hand.
"That is not
a pretty place.
That is our dis-asteroid.
It should *not*
be full of water.
There should be
highways and byways
below all the skyways."

Mr. Hop thinks.
"Everything is flooded,"
he says at last.
"And that means
that the pigeon folk
who live here
have nowhere to land."
Commander Toad
looks out again.
This time he understands.
"I wonder how long
they have been flying."

Doc Peeper looks out
another peephole.
"I will have to treat
a lot of cases
of tired wings," he says.
He gets out a box
of slings and splints.

27

Commander Toad
holds up his hand.
"We must coast down
in our sky skimmer
and scout this watery world."

Lieutenant Lily,
Mr. Hop,
old Doc Peeper
and Commander Toad
buckle on their
special suits
and step in the skimmer.
Then they float
down, down, down, down,
down to the water below.

A big pigeon
in a three-cornered hat
and a fancy sash
perches on the skimmer.
"Salutes and happy
all and to one,"
says the pigeon.
"Mayor Dove here.
You—who?"

"Yoo-hoo to you, too,"
says Commander Toad.
He turns to Mr. Hop.
"He makes no more sense
than the message.
What does he mean?"
"I think he means hello,"
says Mr. Hop.

"To our marble in space
we say come well,"
says Mayor Dove.
"What does he mean?"
asks Commander Toad.
"I think he means
welcome,"
says Mr. Hop.

33

"Why does he talk
in that funny way?"
asks Lieutenant Lily.
"He speaks pigeon,"
says Mr. Hop.
"And we speak toad.
He does not know
our language
very well.

So when he tries
to talk with us
he makes up
something
that is halfway
in-between.
I guess we
could call it
pigeon-toad."

"Help!" says Mayor Dove.
"What does he mean now?"
asks Lieutenant Lily.
"I think he means
HELP!"
says Mr. Hop.

"Do not worry,"
says Commander Toad.
"I am a hero.
I am here to help.
We have brought you
a whole hold
full of swell new beans.

We have:
   Black beans,
   French beans,
   Green beans,
   Jelly beans,
   Jumping beans,
   Runner beans,
   String beans,
   Yellow beans.
They come from
Star Fleet."
"All beans swell,"
says Mayor Dove.
"Yes, they are nice,"
says Commander Toad.

"No, they swell,"
says Mayor Dove.
"Very nice,"
Commander Toad
agrees once more.
"Swell, swell, swell,"
screams Mayor Dove.
He flaps his wings
and shakes his head
and pulls feathers
from his tail.

Commander Toad
turns to Mr. Hop.
"What does he mean?"
"I think he means
that beans swell."
"Oh *swell!*"
says Lieutenant Lily,
shaking her head.

"I mean they swell—
they get bigger in water,"
says Mr. Hop.
"Oh," says Commander Toad,
"they swell!"
He turns back
to Mayor Dove.

42

He holds out his arms—
wide, wider,
then w i d e r still.
"Swell," says Commander Toad.

Mayor Dove smiles.

He explains.

"Rain come.

Beans swell.

Make plugs.

Plug drains.

We fly.

No swim.

Call help.

Water stay.

We go.

Go up.

Wings hurt.

Help."

"Got all that?"
asks Commander Toad,
turning to Mr. Hop.
Mr. Hop
scratches his head.
He thinks deep thoughts
behind his green face.

45

"This world must have
a lot of holes
where all the rain water
goes down.
Those holes
are now plugged up
by swollen beans.
Before the world
was flooded
Mayor Dove
called for help.
But Star Fleet
did not understand
pigeon-toad.

COOPS
&
CONDOS

They got the message
upside-down
and wrong-side around.
The pigeon folk
do not need more beans.
They need a hero,
a hero who can swim
and who can go
under the water
and burst
the swollen beans."

Commander Toad
examines his webbed feet.
He checks his pocket knife.
He blows his nose.
"You look worried,"
says Lieutenant Lily.
"It is time to worry,"
says Commander Toad.

He takes a deep breath.
He holds his nose.
He jumps over
the skimmer's side.
He sinks
down, down, down, down,
down beneath the waves.
The water is cool
and little fish swim
between buildings,
around trees,
over statues
and along roads.

Commander Toad
follows a road
until he sees
a group of enormous beans
swollen as big as
hot air balloons.

He takes out
his Star Fleet pocket knife
and drills a hole
in each bean.
WHOOOOOOOOSH!
The air comes out
and the beans are flat.

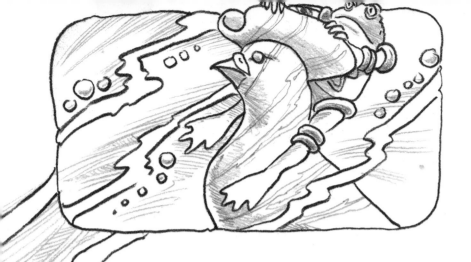

They disappear
down the drains.
Commander Toad
looks worried.
He swims to a statue
of Mayor Dove
and wraps his arms
around its hat.
He knows that soon
all the water
will follow the flat beans
down the drain.

The water will go
fast, faster,
then faster still
and everything in the world
not nailed down
will go down the drains, too.

Crates and carts
float by.
Bottles and bags
float by.
Carriages and couches
and chairs
all whirl along the roads
and disappear
down the drains.

First Commander Toad's head
is out of the water.
Then his belly.
Then his feet.
Soon the statue
is high and dry.
Commander Toad
cannot climb down.
And he cannot fly
without his ship.
"Now I am a *real* hero,"
he says to himself,
"because I am *real* worried."

He calls for help.
Mayor Dove flies down.
"Worry not you,"
coos Mayor Dove.
He picks
Commander Toad
off the statue
and carries him gently
to the ground.

"I am not worried,"
says Commander Toad.
"I am a hero.
A hero tells *other folk*
when to worry."
"You hero true,"
says Mayor Dove.
Lieutenant Lily
and Mr. Hop
sail the sky skimmer
down to rest.

"But what do we do
with all those beans
in our hold?"
asks Lieutenant Lily.
"Need only one kind bean
on this world,"
says Mayor Dove.
"And what kind is that?"
asks Mr. Hop.
"You kind bean.
Amphi-bean!"
He laughs
and slaps his leg
with his wing.

"Amphi-bean?"
says Commander Toad.
"It is not on our list."
Mayor Dove points to
Commander Toad.
He points to the webs
between his toes
and to a puddle nearby.
"Amphi-bean,"
says Mayor Dove.
"He means
an amphibian,"
says Mr. Hop.

"Frogs and toads
are amphibians.
We can go on water
as easily as land."
"Amphi-bean!"
says Commander Toad.
He laughs.
"And we don't swell!"
Mayor Dove
pins a medal
made of feathers
on Commander Toad.

"Come well," he says,
"many times."
"I will come well,"
says Commander Toad,
"only if you promise
no more beans."
"Next year spinach,"
says Mayor Dove.
"Worry not you.
See—I hero, too."

They give hero hugs
and hero salutes.
Then Commander Toad,
brave and bright,
bright and brave,
steps into the skimmer.
The skimmer lifts off
and flies back up
to the *Star Warts*.
"So long,"
shouts Commander Toad
to the pigeons below.
"It has bean fun."
Everyone groans.

"Now all we have to worry about
is where to deliver
all those beans,"
says Commander Toad.
They climb aboard
the long green ship.
It takes off
into deep hopper space
and leapfrogs
across the galaxy
from star to star to star.

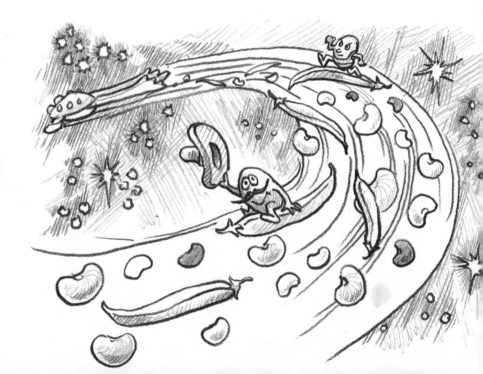

3